Mish Mash Hash

You can read more stories about
the animals from Potter's Barn
by collecting the rest of the series.

For a complete list, look at
the back of the book.

Mish Mash Hash

Francesca Simon

Illustrated by Emily Bolam

Orion
Children's Books

Mish Mash Hash first appeared in *Moo Baa Baa Quack*,
first published in Great Britain in 1997
by Orion Children's Books
This edition first published in Great Britain in 2011
by Orion Children's Books
a division of the Orion Publishing Group Ltd
Orion House
5 Upper St Martin's Lane
London WC2H 9EA
An Hachette UK Company

1 3 5 7 9 10 8 6 4 2

A catalogue record for this book is available from the British Library.

ISBN 978 1 4440 0207 2

Printed in China

The Orion Publishing Group's policy is to use papers that are natural,
renewable and recyclable products made from wood grown in sustainable forests.
The logging and manufacturing processes are expected to conform
to the environmental regulations of the country of origin.

www.orionbooks.co.uk

For Steven Butler,
my favourite off-piste chef

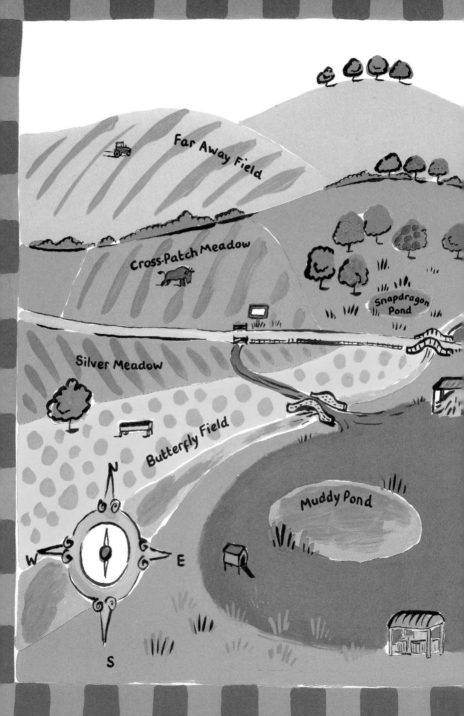

Hello from everyone

Squeaky the cat

Miaow

Henny-Penny

Cluck
Cluck

The chicks

Cheep
Cheep

at Potter's Barn!

MOOOO

Daffodil the cow

Rosie the calf

Father Goat

Bleat

Billy the Kid

Mother Sheep

Baaaaa

Tilly and Tam
the lambs

Mother Duck

Quack
Quack

Five Ducklings

Neigh

Trot the horse

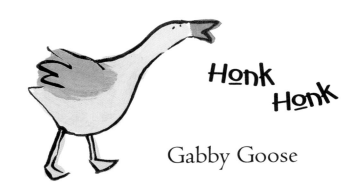

Honk Honk

Gabby Goose

Woof

Buster the dog

Oink oink

Belle the pig

Cock-a-doodle-doo!

Red Rooster

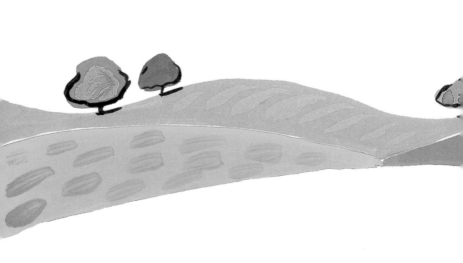

Welcome to Potter's Barn!

The sun always shines and the fun
never stops at Potter's Barn Farm.
Join the animals on their adventures
as they sing, stomp, make cakes,
get lost, run off, and go wild.

Making a cake for Belle
was Gabby's idea.

"Belle works so hard conducting the Potter's Barn Band," said Gabby. "It would be a lovely surprise for her."

"She's gone to the Big Woods with Buster this morning," said Rosie the calf. "If we hurry, we can have the cake ready before she gets back."

"Who knows how to make a cake?"
said Henny-Penny.

No one spoke.

"It seems to me," said Daffodil,
"that grass tastes extremely nice."

"You can't go wrong with oats,"
said Trot.

"Worms and beetles are my
best treat," said Red Rooster.

"Flies and seeds can't be beat,"
said the ducks.

"My food is the tastiest,"
said Tam.

"No, ours,"
said the hens.

"No, mine,"
said Squeaky.

"I know," said Tilly. "Let's mix our favourite foods together. That way our cake will taste extra yummy!"

32

Everyone thought this was
a great idea and ran off to
collect the ingredients.

Into the bucket went:

beetles

thistles

oats

seeds

leaves

hay

slugs

worms

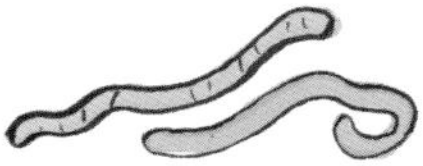

flies

plants

grass

ants

milk

and

spiders

"How about some nice cardboard?"
said Billy the Kid.

"Yuck!" squealed Gabby.

"It was just an idea,"
said Billy.

"Now, mix!" shouted Tam.

Swish Swash Slosh
Swish Swash Slosh

Round and round and round
they stirred, until at last
the cake was mixed.

"Hmmm, doesn't that look
delicious?" said the ducklings.

"I can't wait to taste it," said Rosie.

"Now," said Gabby Goose.
"We'll turn the cake out onto the
ground and then decorate it."

Slowly and carefully, the animals
tipped the bucket over.

Slip Slop Slip Slop... Plop!

The cake slopped out of
the bucket into a heap
on the ground.

"Oh no!" wailed the lambs.

"Our lovely cake!"
peeped the chicks.

"Why didn't it keep its shape?"
moaned Gabby.

"Never mind," said Trot.
"We've made something
better than a cake. We've made
Mish Mash Hash."

"Quick, Belle's coming,"
said Squeaky.

They decorated the Mish Mash
Hash as fast as they could.

Belle wandered into the farmyard.
"What's going on?" she said.

"Surprise!"
shouted the animals.

"It's for you, Belle," said Gabby.
"Thank you for all your hard work."

Belle smiled and smiled and smiled.
Then she took a mouthful.

"Wow!" said Belle.
"Tastes great! What is it?"

"Mish Mash Hash,"
said Gabby.

"Can I have the recipe?"
said Belle.

"Sure," said Trot.
"You add…

oats

 seeds

leaves

 hay

slugs

worms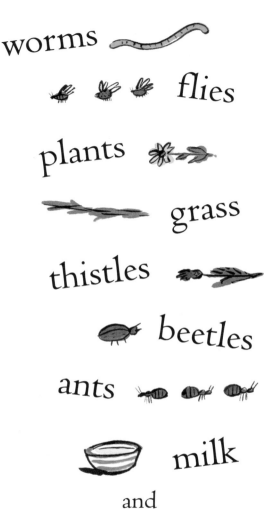

flies

plants

grass

thistles

beetles

ants

milk

and

spiders

"Stir! Slop! Eat!"

Oink
follow me

Did you enjoy
Mish Mash Hash?
Can you remember the
things that happened?

Whose idea is it to make Belle a cake?

Why do the animals decide
to make Belle a cake?

Who likes worms and beetles best?

What does Tilly think will
make the cake extra yummy?

What happens when the animals
turn the cake out onto the ground?

What does Trot decide to call
their cake?

What does Belle say when
she eats the cake?

What goes into the Mish Mash Hash?

For more farmyard fun with the
animals at Potter's Barn, look out
for the other books in the series.

Runaway
Duckling

Where are
my Lambs?

Billy The Kid
Goes Wild

Barnyard
Hullabaloo

Chicks Just
Want to
Have Fun

Moo Baa
Baa Quack